How to Grow a
MONSTER

by Kiki Thorpe
illustrated by Barbara Bongini

Kane Press
New York

For Roxie and Freddie—K.T.

To my mom and my dad for their
support—B.B.

Library of Congress Cataloging-in-Publication Data
Names: Thorpe, Kiki, author. | Bongini, Barbara, illustrator.
Title: How to grow a monster / by Kiki Thorpe ; illustrated by Barbara Bongini.
Description: New York : Kane Press, 2020. | Summary: After a summer of too much
zucchini, Gabe and his sister are determined to keep that vegetable out of their garden, but
something monstrous is hiding under the leaves. Includes facts about zucchini and gardening.
Identifiers: LCCN 2019011847 (print) | LCCN 2019015290 (ebook) |
ISBN 9781635922783 (ebook) | ISBN 9781635922776 (pbk) | ISBN 9781635922769
(reinforced library binding)
Subjects: | CYAC: Gardening—Fiction. | Zucchini—Fiction. | Brothers and sisters.
Classification: LCC PZ7.T3974 (ebook) | LCC PZ7.T3974 Hs 2020 (print) |
DDC [E]—dc23
LC record available at https://lccn.loc.gov/2019011847

10 9 8 7 6 5 4 3 2 1

Kane Press

An imprint of Boyds Mills & Kane, a division of Astra Publishing House

www.kanepress.com

Printed in the United States of America

Makers Make It Work is a registered trademark of Astra Publishing House

It was spring. The sun was shining. A warm breeze blew. Mom was wearing a funny hat.

I knew it was that time of year again—time to plant the garden!

Every year my sister, Kara, and I helped Mom plant our garden. My favorite part was digging in the dirt.

Mom got out trowels, gardening forks, and seeds. "What should we plant first?" she asked.

I looked through the seed packets. There were carrots, lettuce, radishes, peas, and— "Oh, no!" I groaned. "Not zucchini again!"

Last summer, we grew tons of zucchini. We didn't know what to do with it all. Mom put it in everything—zucchini pancakes, zucchini noodles, zucchini loaf. Zucchini for breakfast, lunch, and dinner!

Just thinking about it made me feel green.

"Don't worry, Gabe. It'll just be a few plants,"
Mom said.

"That's what she told us last year, too," Kara
mumbled.

While Mom was looking for her gardening gloves, Kara pulled me aside. "This year, we are going to take care of those zucchini before they take over," she said. "I have a plan."

A plan? I liked the sound of that!

Kara whispered in my ear. Then we got to work.

Zucchini like lots of sun. Kara and I tried to plant the seeds in the shady part of the garden. We figured with less sun, the zucchini plants wouldn't grow as well.

Some plants need a lot of sun to thrive. Other plants do better in shade. Read your seed packets to see where your plants will do best.

But Mom noticed. "Zucchini go over here!" She pointed to a sunny spot. *Drat.*

"Don't worry," Kara whispered. "I have a plan B."

Kara and I were extra helpful in the garden. Every day, we weeded and watered. But really we were spies. We were keeping an eye on the zucchini.

Pulling up seedlings to make room for larger plants is called *thinning*, and it can help your garden. It gives the remaining plants more room to grow.

A single zucchini plant can produce more than six pounds of zucchini in one season!

When the plants sprouted, it was time for action. Kara and I pulled up some of the seedlings. Not all of them, mind you. We left a few for Mom.

"Four plants seem like plenty," Kara said. I had to agree.

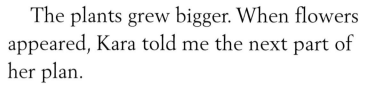

The plants grew bigger. When flowers appeared, Kara told me the next part of her plan.

"Zucchini plants have two different kinds of flowers," she explained. "I read about it in Mom's gardening book. The first kind of flowers pollinate the second kind. That's why we have to pick these flowers. No flowers, no pollination. No pollination, no zucchini!"

Pollination is when pollen is shifted from the male part of the plant to the female part. Usually the pollen is moved by wind, birds, or insects, such as bees.

"Won't Mom be mad if we pick them?"
I asked.

"Not if we make dinner with them," Kara
said. "That's the cool part—you can eat
zucchini blossoms!"

Kara and I harvested the flowers.

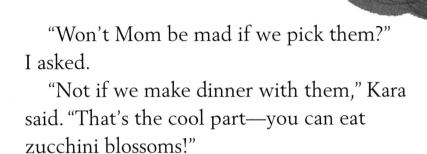

Harvest means to pick
or gather a crop.

Kara found a recipe online. We made
zucchini blossom quesadillas for dinner.

Mom was really impressed. "What a treat!"
she said. "I had no idea you two were such
gourmet chefs."

"Have seconds," Kara said.
I thought eating flowers would be weird.
But they actually tasted pretty good.

Kara and I thought our zucchini troubles were over. But a week later, I spotted some small green zucchini on the plants.

"Uh-oh!" I said. "We must have missed some flowers."

"Quick, pick them before they get any bigger!" Kara said.

Just then, Mom showed up. "What's going on?" she asked.

Kara held out the little zucchini. "Look . . . it's, uh, the first crop."

Mom looked surprised. "I've never known you two to be so excited to eat zucchini," she said.

"Better a few small zucchini now than zillions of zucchini later," Kara whispered.

Kara's not exactly right here. Picking early might actually encourage a zucchini plant to grow more!

For the best flavor, pick zucchini when they are small.

We had the little zucchini for dinner that night. Mom cooked them in butter. Hmm, not bad. Maybe I was starting to like zucchini after all!

I thought that would be the end of it. But a few weeks later, I noticed something hiding under the leaves of a zucchini plant.

It was big. It was green. It was—yikes!

"It's a monster!" I yelled.

Kara and Mom came running. There, beneath the leaves, was the biggest zucchini we had ever seen!

Kara grabbed the garden shears. She was about to cut the giant zucchini from the vine. "Stop!" I shouted.

"What's wrong?" Kara asked.

"Nothing's wrong," I said. "It's awesome!"
That monster zucchini was the coolest thing
I'd ever seen in our garden. I couldn't let Kara
cut it.

"I'm going to call it the Green Zuke Monster," I said. "Greenie for short."

"You named the zucchini?" Kara rolled her eyes. "Oh, brother."

How big could a zucchini get? I had to find out.

Mom helped me do some gardening research. Kara and I had created a monster without even knowing it. We thinned the seedlings. We harvested the small, early zucchini. It turns out that's how we helped grow a giant zucchini.

For the rest of the summer, I took care of my monster. I watered the zucchini plant every week. When the weather was hot, I watered more often.

Not all plants need the same amount of water. Celery needs a lot of water or the stalks will taste bitter. A desert plant, such as a cactus, needs much less water.

When I saw bugs on the leaves, I picked them off.

I planted marigolds nearby to help keep other pests away from the garden.

Marigolds are natural pest control. They put out a chemical that fights off some tiny worms that feed on plant roots.

And every day, I measured. One day, Greenie
grew two whole inches!

By late August, Greenie was over two feet long. It weighed almost fifteen pounds! I was super proud of my monster.

Kara wasn't as excited. "We're going to be eating zucchini lasagna for months," she grumbled.

"Actually," Mom said. "I have a better idea."

We took Greenie to the county fair instead.
My zucchini won first prize!
"Way to go, little bro," Kara said.

I can't wait for next summer. I have big plans. I'm going to grow a whole garden of MONSTERS!

Learn Like a Maker

When you plant a vegetable garden, you get to eat what you grow. That's great . . . unless your mom plants something you don't like. But by trying to keep Mom's zucchini in check, Kara and Gabe became better gardeners than they could have imagined!

Look Back

- Reread page 9. Do you think the plan to plant the zucchini in the shade would have worked? Why or why not?

- On page 12, Kara says, "No flowers, no pollination. No pollination, no zucchini!" What is pollination and why is it important?

Try This!

Throwing Shade

Test out Kara's idea. Does putting a plant that likes sun in a shady place keep it from growing as well?

You will need:
- A packet of green bean or daisy seeds
- 2 pots
- Potting soil
- A watering can
- A ruler
- A notebook

1. In each pot, plant the same number of seeds in the same amount of soil.

2. Place one pot in an area that is shaded most of the day. Place the other in a spot that gets lots of sun.

3. Give the plants the same amount of water.

4. Measure the height of each plant. Keep notes on how many vegetables each plant produces or how many flowers bloom.

How do the two plants compare? Do you agree with Kara's theory?